POLAR BEARS

MEGAN BORGERT-SPANIOL

An Imprint of Abdo Publishing
abdobooks.com

ABDOBOOKS.COM

Published by Abdo Publishing, a division of ABDO, PO Box 398166, Minneapolis, Minnesota 55439.

Printed in the United States of America, North Mankato, Minnesota
102018
012019

Design and Production: Mighty Media, Inc.
Editor: Liz Salzmann
Cover Photographs: Shutterstock
Interior Photographs: AP Images, p. 26; iStockphoto, pp. 9, 19, 25, 28; Shutterstock, pp. 4, 5, 7, 11, 12, 15, 16–17, 20, 23, 29

Library of Congress Control Number: 2018949394

Publisher's Cataloging-in-Publication Data
Names: Borgert-Spaniol, Megan, author.
Title: Polar bears / by Megan Borgert-Spaniol.
Description: Minneapolis, Minnesota : Abdo Publishing, 2019 | Series: Arctic animals at risk | Includes online resources and index.
Identifiers: ISBN 9781532116995 (lib. bdg.) | ISBN 9781532159831 (ebook)
Subjects: LCSH: Polar bear--Juvenile literature. | Polar bear--Behavior--Juvenile literature. | Environmental protection--Arctic regions--Juvenile literature. | Habitat protection--Juvenile literature.
Classification: DDC 599.786--dc23

TABLE OF CONTENTS

CHAPTER 1

RULERS OF THE ARCTIC ICE

The Arctic landscape is still and quiet. Thick layers of sea ice float atop steely blue water for miles on end. Near the edge of the ice, a polar bear's head breaks the surface of the water.

The 1,000-pound (450 kg) predator pushes its body up onto the sea ice. It shakes the cold water off its thick coat and rolls in the snow to dry off. Then, it begins a slow stroll across the ice.

Hungry, the polar bear sniffs the air. The polar bear's keen sense of smell leads it to a hole in the sea ice. It is a breathing hole made by a seal, the polar bear's most common prey. In time, a seal will surface here for air. When it does, the polar bear will be ready to attack.

There are about 26,000 polar bears in the world.

POLAR BEARS AT RISK

Polar bears are in the family Ursidae. This family also includes brown bears and American black bears. But unlike its land-dwelling relatives, the polar bear is considered a marine mammal. Polar bears spend most of their lives on or in the waters of the Arctic Ocean. They live along the northern coastlines of the United States, Canada, Greenland, Norway, and Russia.

Polar bears rule the sea ice of their Arctic **habitats**. But these powerful predators are in trouble. Human activities, such as oil exploration and industrial shipping, threaten polar bear habitats. However, the greatest threat to polar bear habitats is climate change.

WHAT IS CLIMATE CHANGE?

Climate change is periodic change in Earth's weather patterns. In recent years, scientists have observed an increase in the rate of climate change. Most scientists agree this is due to humans burning **fossil fuels**. Burning fossil fuels produces **greenhouse gases** which trap heat in Earth's atmosphere. This has led to rising global temperatures.

Polar bears rely on sea ice for hunting seals and other prey. But as Earth's climate gets warmer, sea ice is melting. Polar bears are losing their hunting grounds along with the prey they need to survive. Many polar bears in the northern extremes of the Arctic have not yet experienced much sea ice loss. But if the current rate of climate change continues, all polar bears will eventually feel its effects.

CHAPTER 3

DENNING AND CUBS

Sea ice is not only a hunting ground for polar bears. It also serves as a breeding ground. In spring, males sniff out females' scent trails on the sea ice to find mates. Soon after mating, males and females part ways.

Over the summer, females fill up on fatty prey to prepare for the upcoming denning season. This is a period during fall and winter when **pregnant** polar bears enter a state of rest. It is during this time that females give birth.

To prepare their dens, females dig small caves into snow banks or hills. They enter their dens in late fall. Around December, denning females give birth to one to three cubs. Twin cubs are most common.

Newborn polar bears are about 12 inches (30 cm) long, blind, and toothless. Their mothers keep them warm and provide milk. For the next several months, denning mothers do not eat or drink. While their cubs nurse, mothers sleep and survive on stored fat.

Mothers and their cubs emerge from their dens in March or April. However, cubs remain with their mothers for two to three years.

Cubs gain weight quickly. A mother polar bear's milk is 33 percent fat!

During this time, the cubs learn how to hunt, swim, and survive. By the time they are fully grown, polar bears are masters of their Arctic homes!

COMMANDING THE COLD

Polar bears thrive in a climate few other animals can withstand. In the northern reaches of the polar bear's range, winter temperatures average –29 degrees Fahrenheit (–34°C). However, temperatures can drop to –50 degrees Fahrenheit (–46°C)!

Polar bears are well adapted to the cold. Three layers of **insulation** keeps them comfortable in the harsh climate. The polar bear's outermost defense against the cold is its two-layered coat.

The coat has a top layer of long, hollow guard hairs. These hairs are transparent. But because they are hollow, they reflect light and appear white. Guard hairs trap warm air to insulate the bear's body. A softer undercoat also traps heat against the bear's skin.

A polar bear's skin is also adapted to the cold. Although the creature appears white, the skin beneath its coat is black. The dark color allows it to absorb the sun's heat which warms the bear's body. Beneath the skin is a layer of fat up to 4 inches (10 cm) thick. This fat is the polar bear's innermost layer of defense against the cold.

This warm **insulation** is especially useful in the cold Arctic waters. Polar bears often swim to find food. And although they are large, these bears move through water with ease. This is partly due to their

A polar bear's coat can change color depending on its diet. Eating a lot of seals can turn the bear's fur yellow from the seals' oils.

large, flat front paws. Slightly **webbed** and up to 12 inches (30 cm) wide, these paws are perfect for paddling.

As polar bears swim, their body fat keeps them warm and **buoyant**. Their hollow guard hairs also help them stay afloat. Meanwhile, natural oils on their coats keep water out. This keeps the bears **insulated** by trapped air, even as they swim!

Although polar bears are at home in the water, they spend much of their time on sea ice. Their bodies are well adapted to walking on this cold, slippery surface. Polar bears have black pads on the bottom of their paws. These pads are covered in small bumps that grip the ice. This keeps the bears from slipping.

A polar bear's large, wide paws help it tread on thin ice without breaking it. And a polar bear moves differently on especially thin ice. The bear lowers its body and extends its legs farther apart. This **distributes** the bear's weight over a larger area of ice. Doing so places less pressure on any one area of thin ice.

Polar bears can swim for several hours at a time. They swim at about 6 miles per hour (10 kmh).

SEA ICE HUNTERS

Polar bears are at the top of the Arctic food chain. They have no natural predators. But this doesn't mean getting enough food is easy. A polar bear needs to eat an average of 4.5 pounds (2 kg) of fat per day. Polar bears spend more than half their time hunting for food.

Polar bears are expert hunters. Because of their size, they can take down large prey, such as walruses and beluga whales. Polar bears have also been known to eat birds' eggs, berries, and land mammals. However, polar bears primarily hunt ringed and bearded seals. These animals provide the fat that polar bears need to survive.

Polar bears cannot swim fast enough to catch seals in open water. Instead, the bears wait near the edges of sea ice for seals to surface. The predators also sniff out breathing holes that seals cut into the ice. Polar bears may wait for hours or even days for seals to surface. When they do, the polar bears pounce!

Polar bears also stalk seals that are resting on sea ice. To do this, a polar bear moves slowly toward a seal. If the seal raises its head, the

Sometimes polar bears only eat the fat from seals. They leave the rest of the seals for other animals to eat.

bear stops, relying on its white coat for camouflage. Once the bear is within about 20 feet (6 m) of the seal, it attacks. In short bursts, polar bears can run up to 25 miles per hour (40 kmh)!

In the northern Arctic, polar bears can hunt on sea ice year-round. But the southern areas of their range often have seasonal sea ice. As temperatures rise each summer, sea ice in these regions begins to melt.

Without sea ice, polar bears cannot hunt their most important source of food. So, most polar bears swim north to where the sea ice has not melted. These bears may swim hundreds of miles in pursuit of sea ice and prey.

Not all polar bears make this exhausting journey. Some come ashore and spend warmer months on the coasts of the Arctic Ocean. These bears face months of little to no food. During this period, polar bears get energy from stored body fat. They can survive this way for seven to eight months.

Polar bears swim near the surface of the water. They can also dive to catch prey.

CHAPTER 6

DECLINE OF SEA ICE

Polar bears can survive without sea ice and seals for long stretches of time. But climate change is pushing polar bears beyond their fasting limits. This is because rising global temperatures are melting Arctic sea ice.

Since 1979, scientists at NASA have been observing Arctic sea ice using **satellite** data. The data shows this sea ice has been shrinking over the past 35 years. In 2012, it hit a record low. Rising temperatures are causing sea ice to melt sooner each spring and form later each fall. This leaves polar bears with less time to hunt the food they need.

Polar bears in regions with seasonal sea ice are the most threatened. As sea ice disappears, the bears must survive longer periods of fasting onshore. Or, they must swim greater distances in pursuit of sea ice and seals. These long trips are difficult for even the healthiest polar bears.

Between 2004 and 2009, scientists tracked the movements of more than 60 female polar bears. One tracked bear swam

Polar bears live in remote areas, so it is hard for scientists to study them. But scientists are working hard to study how climate change may affect polar bears.

426 miles (685 km) before finding a resting place. During that swim, she lost 22 percent of her body weight. Her cub did not survive the journey.

Cases like this show that young polar bears and weak adults are less likely to survive long swims. Those that do survive burn up much of their body fat. This leaves the bears with less energy and **insulation** against the cold. Such conditions threaten a polar bear's ability to reproduce and survive.

Melting sea ice brings another possible threat to polar bears. Shrinking sea ice has opened Arctic waters for use by humans. Industrial activities, such as offshore oil drilling and shipping, are expected to increase as sea ice is reduced. These activities increase the risk of Arctic oil spills.

A large oil spill in Arctic waters could be **devastating**. It could **contaminate** the Arctic **habitat** and **food chain**, possibly killing the prey that polar bears depend on. Polar bears would also be at risk of swallowing toxic oil as they try to clean their fur.

Such an oil spill has not yet occurred in Arctic waters. Because of this, there are no proven methods for cleaning an Arctic oil spill. A lack of emergency preparedness could result in widespread harm.

Being exposed to oil from spills could cause organ failure and brain damage in polar bears.

IMPORTANCE OF POLAR BEARS

An Arctic oil spill could be a huge problem for polar bears. However, the ongoing loss of sea ice presents the most severe consequences. If polar bears can't hunt seals, they may rely solely on land-based plants and animals. This could reduce the food sources that land predators, such as wolves and Arctic foxes, need to survive.

On land, polar bears are also attracted to smells of food and trash coming from human communities. This increases the likelihood that humans and polar bears will come into contact. Such conflict can be deadly for both humans and the bears.

Polar bears' fight for survival affects other animals and even humans. But what happens if polar bears die off? As the top predators of their ecosystem, polar bears affect the populations of seals and other prey. They also indirectly affect the populations of fish and other organisms that seals prey on. Without polar bears, the Arctic ecosystem would dramatically change.

Based on the rate of sea ice loss, experts **predict** the fate of polar bears. They believe two-thirds of the global polar bear population could be gone by 2050. Scientists emphasize the need to act against climate change. Without such action, they say, wild polar bears could be extinct within 100 years.

To maintain its weight and energy, a polar bear must eat one adult seal every ten days.

SAVING POLAR BEARS

Scientists' warnings about the fate of polar bears have become more urgent in recent years. They argue that action must be taken now to save polar bears' future. One of the first steps in protecting a species is the official recognition of its threatened **status**.

In 2006 and 2008, the International Union for the Conservation of Nature (IUCN) listed polar bears as **Vulnerable**. This means the species is facing a high risk of extinction in the wild. The IUCN recommends certain actions to protect polar bears. However, it is up to individual countries to pass laws that assure this protection.

IUCN

The International Union for the Conservation of Nature is a global authority on the status of wildlife. It collects scientific data and experts' studies to determine the status of a species. Then, governments and conservation organizations use this information to make decisions about species protection.

The Endangered Species Act does not include any regulations on greenhouse gas emissions to help save polar bears.

In 2008, the US Fish and Wildlife Service listed polar bears as a threatened species under the **Endangered** Species Act (ESA). This action officially recognized that polar bears are at risk of becoming endangered. It also gave the species certain protections against hunting and **habitat** destruction.

However, many argue that such laws alone are not enough to save polar bears. Scientists and wildlife supporters argue that to preserve polar bear **habitats**, climate change must be halted. This requires

In 2009, a sculpture of a polar bear on an iceberg was placed in the River Thames in London, England. It raised awareness about climate change and melting sea ice.

passing laws that limit **greenhouse gas** emissions. Supporters also argue that polar bear **habitats** should be protected from industrial activities, such as oil drilling.

Enacting such policies is difficult. **Fossil fuels** are important energy resources in many nations, including the United States. Many officials argue that reducing fossil fuel production would harm any economy that relies on them.

Still, conservation groups are doing what they can to protect polar bears. In 2015, representatives from countries in the polar bear's range approved a joint conservation effort. It is called the Circumpolar Action Plan for Polar Bears (CAP). The CAP aims to manage, research, and observe polar bear populations. It also plans to communicate to lawmakers the importance of reducing greenhouse gas emissions.

Global **nonprofits**, such as Polar Bears International, have similar goals. Such organizations encourage the public to help protect polar bears and other animals at risk. People can do so by volunteering or giving money. With immediate action, polar bears can once again **thrive** in their Arctic kingdom!

POLAR BEAR
FACT SHEET

SCIENTIFIC NAME: ***Ursus maritimus***

LENGTH: **7.25 to 8 feet (2.2 to 2.4 m)**

WEIGHT: **900 to 1,600 pounds (408 to 726 kg)**

DIET: **carnivore**

AVERAGE LIFESPAN IN THE WILD: **25 to 30 years**

IUCN STATUS: **Vulnerable**

WHAT CAN YOU DO?

You can take action to help polar bears and other Arctic animals at risk!

- Give money to or volunteer for polar bear conservation organizations. These include World Wildlife Fund, Defenders of Wildlife, and Polar Bears International.

- Write to local lawmakers asking them to support policies that protect polar bears. These policies include laws that limit **greenhouse gas** emissions.

- Tell your friends and family about climate change and how it affects Arctic wildlife such as polar bears.

- Reduce your use of **fossil fuels** by choosing to bike, walk, or take the bus instead of riding in a car.

GLOSSARY

buoyant—able to float.

contaminate—to make unfit for use by adding something harmful or unpleasant.

devastating—causing great damage or harm.

distribute—to spread out over an area.

enact—to make into law.

endangered—in danger of becoming extinct.

food chain—the order in which plants and animals feed on each other.

fossil fuel—a fuel formed in the earth from the remains of plants or animals. Coal, oil, and natural gas are fossil fuels.

greenhouse gas—a gas, such as carbon dioxide, that traps heat in Earth's atmosphere.

habitat—a place where a living thing is naturally found.

insulate—to keep something from losing heat. Insulation is something that prevents a loss of heat.

landscape—a large area of scenery.

nonprofit—not existing or carried on for the purpose of making a profit.

predict—to guess something ahead of time on the basis of observation, experience, or reasoning.

pregnant—having one or more babies growing within the body.

satellite—a manufactured object that orbits Earth. It relays scientific information back to Earth.

status—a state or a condition.

thrive—to do well.

urgent—demanding immediate attention or action.

vulnerable—able to be hurt or attacked. An animal has a vulnerable status when it is likely to become endangered.

webbed—having skin connecting the fingers or toes.

ONLINE RESOURCES

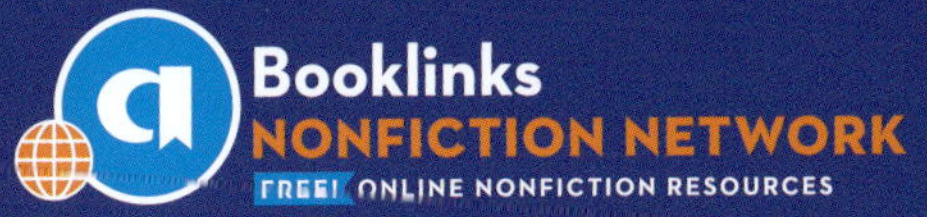

To learn more about polar bears, visit abdobooklinks.com. These links are routinely monitored and updated to provide the most current information available.

INDEX